Text copyright © 2003 by Rindert Kromhout
Illustrations copyright © 2003 by Annemarie van Haeringen
English translation copyright © 2006 by North-South Books Inc., New York

First published in the Netherlands by Uitgeverij Leopold Amsterdam,
under the title *Kleine Ezel en de oppas*.

Published in the United States, Great Britain, Canada, Australia, and New Zealand in 2006
by North-South Books, an imprint of NordSüd Verlag AG, Gossau Zürich, Switzerland.

Distributed in the United States by North-South Books Inc., New York.
Library of Congress Cataloging-in-Publication Data is available.
A CIP catalogue record for this book is available from The British Library.

ISBN-13: 978-0-7358-2057-9
ISBN-10: 0-7358-2057-0

10 9 8 7 6 5 4 3 2 1

Printed in Belgium

By Rindert Kromhout

LITTLE DONKEY AND THE BABY-SITTER

Illustrated by
Annemarie van Haeringen

Translated by
Marianne Martens

North-South Books
New York/London

Mama Donkey was going out to see a film with Billy Goat,
so Nanny Hen came to stay with Little Donkey.

"Don't go," said Little Donkey.
"I won't be long," promised Mama Donkey.
  Little Donkey thought for a moment.
"I'm a big donkey," he said. "I can stay by myself."
 "Absolutely not," said Mama Donkey. "Now give me a hug,
  and be a good boy with Nanny Hen."

"Hello, little one," said Nanny Hen, making herself comfortable on the couch. "We're going to have a lovely evening together."
Little Donkey poured the tea.

"How would you like a nice bowl of oatmeal?" asked Nanny Hen.

"No, thank you. I want fries, please," said Little Donkey.

"Fries?" said Nanny Hen. "Mama didn't say anything about fries."

"Mama always lets me have fries," said Little Donkey.

Nanny Hen decided to have something tasty to eat too.

She opened the cupboard and took out a big hunk of cheese.

"Mama says you're not allowed to eat the cheese," said Little Donkey.

But Nanny Hen ate the whole thing anyway.

"Tell me a story, please," said Little Donkey.

"Okay, one bedtime story," said Nanny Hen. "Once upon a time, there was a tired little donkey who brushed his teeth and got ready for bed as quickly as he could. He couldn't wait to get into his nice, comfortable bed."

Little Donkey didn't like Nanny Hen's story.

"I want to play outside," he said.

"Oh, it's much too late for that," said Nanny Hen.

"Mama always lets me," said Little Donkey.

"Well, all right then," said Nanny Hen. "Just for a little while."

Little Donkey ran outside.

"Jackie!" he shouted.

"Little Donkey!" shouted Jackie. "My mama has to run an errand, so I'm coming out to play with you!"

They ran through the garden, jumped in the mud,
and splashed in the pond.
"Be careful, boys!" shouted Nanny Hen from the window.

Little Donkey got all his toys out.

"What a terrible mess you are making," said Nanny Hen,
 shaking her head.

"Mama always lets me," said Little Donkey, giggling.

"My mama lets me do everything," he said to Jackie.

"So does mine," said Jackie. "She's so nice."

"Jackie! Time to come home!" shouted Jackie's mama.
"Uh-oh!" said Jackie, and off he ran.

Little Donkey sat happily in the grass. He'd had fun with Jackie.

"Now be a good boy and pick up your toys," said Nanny Hen.

"Mama never makes me," said Little Donkey.

Nanny Hen looked at him sternly. "That's enough now.
Time to tidy up."

Little Donkey pouted. "I want my mama," he said.

"I want you to go away."

And just as Little Donkey started to run inside . . .

Ooooowwww! he howled. Little Donkey had fallen down
and banged his knees and his nose.

"Oh dear, did you hurt yourself, little one?"

"Yes," wailed Little Donkey.

"Come and sit with me," said Nanny Hen.

"A chocolate will make me feel better," said Little Donkey.

"And Mama lets you have chocolates?" asked Nanny Hen, winking.

"Oh yes, Mama always lets me," said Little Donkey confidently.

Soon the chocolate was gone, but the pain was still there.

"Perhaps some lemonade would help," said Little Donkey.

"All right then," said Nanny Hen. She had some too, and this time
  Little Donkey didn't mind.

"Story, please," said Little Donkey.

"A story? What should it be about?" said Nanny Hen.

"About a little donkey who fell down," said Little Donkey.

"Okay," said Nanny Hen. "Once upon a time, there was a little donkey who fell down . . . and he hurt himself terribly!" Little Donkey quite liked this story. But he was getting very sleepy. Little Donkey yawned.

"Has Little Donkey been a good boy?" asked Mama Donkey.
Nanny Hen smiled. "Oh yes, he's been a very good boy,"
she said, winking at Mama Donkey.

"Wake up, sleepyhead," said Mama Donkey. "It's bath time."
"Nanny says I don't have to," said Little Donkey.